Shakespeare's Greatest Stories

Abridged and Illustrated

AS YOU LIKE IT

Wonder House

Wonder House

(An imprint of Prakash Books)

contact@wonderhousebooks.com

ISBN : 9789389717761

Cover image: Work of Francis Hayman, taken from https://commons.wikimedia.org/wiki/File:Francis_Hayman_002.jpg

ABOUT THE AUTHOR

William Shakespeare

William Shakespeare is undoubtedly one of the greatest playwrights to have ever lived. He gained fame for his excellent ability to portray human emotions in the form of comedies, tragedies, tragicomedies and historical plays. Some of his greatest plays include *Macbeth, Hamlet, Romeo and Juliet, The Merchant of Venice, A Midsummer Night's Dream, Julius Caesar, As You Like It, Othello, The Tempest*, and many more. He has been credited with giving the world a plethora of new words and phrases, which have enriched the English language.

Popularly known as the 'Bard of Avon', Shakespeare's contributions to literature are numerous and significant. Apart from plays, he also wrote sonnets and poems. Along with being a writer, Shakespeare was also a co-owner of a theatrical company named Lord Chamberlain's Men. Later, he became a co-owner of The Globe Theatre, which was built in 1599. The Globe is still one of the most cherished theatres in the world and manages to put up thrilling productions of Shakespeare's best works even today.

Cast List

As You Like It

Orlando:	Sir Rowland de Bois' youngest son
Duke Senior:	The rightful ruler of the dukedom
Rosalind:	Duke Senior's daughter
Jaques:	A faithful lord of Duke Senior
Celia:	Duke Frederick's daughter
Duke Frederick:	Duke Senior's brother
Touchstone:	A clown
Oliver:	Sir Rowland de Bois' eldest son
Silvius:	A young shepherd
Phoebe:	A young shepherdess
Lord Amiens:	A faithful lord of Duke Senior
Charles:	A professional wrestler
Adam:	Sir Rowland de Bois' former servant
Corin:	A young shepherd
Audrey:	A goatherd

The fool doth think he is wise,
but the wise man knows himself to be a fool.

– **Touchstone**, Act V, Scene 1

Orlando was the youngest, most unfortunate son of the late Sir Rowland de Bois. Upon his father's death, Orlando was left with a thousand crowns, a measly sum for a young man of his age and background. He was also left in the care of his eldest brother, Oliver de Bois.

Oliver inherited virtually everything in his father's estate. However, he disobeyed his father's last wish and neglected his charge as the owner of the estate and the caretaker of his brothers.

Oliver arranged good education for his other brother, Jaques, whereas Orlando was refused education and anything else that was rightfully his.

One day, Orlando confided in Adam, their oldest servant, "Adam, I don't understand what I've done to receive such hatred from my own brother! Oliver confines me at home, away from the life of a gentleman. His horses are treated better than me! At least they receive proper food and training. He gives me plenty of nothing and takes away

everything I have. He forces me to eat with his servants and live without an education. It is troubling to say that my elder brother is my enemy."

Orlando stood up violently. "Adam, I won't stand for it any longer! I thought my brother will change and understand my pride. But he's stubborn. If he doesn't change, I will revolt; though I have no clue how."

Suddenly, Adam warned Orlando that Oliver was approaching. Orlando asked Adam to hide and witness his brother's ruthlessness.

Oliver walked in coolly and asked him, "Brother! What are you doing here?"

"Nothing. I was never taught to do anything!" replied Orlando, sharply.

"Well then, what are you undoing?"

"I am helping you undo one of God's creations—me!"

"Indeed. So find something better to do and get lost."

The brothers got into a scuffle and swords were drawn. Adam stepped in quickly to resolve the fight. "Gentlemen, please calm down, at least in your father's memory!"

Oliver pulled himself free of Orlando's grasp and cried, "Let me go, you pig!"

Orlando spit, "Today, I will speak and you will listen, big brother. After our father's death, you treated me like a germ in the mud. You kept me away from education and proper training, and refused to give me what's rightfully mine! Today, I stand here for my dignity and respect.

You either give me a life fit for my rank or give me my inheritance, so that I can make my fortune elsewhere."

"And when it's gone? What will you do? Beg?" Oliver had heard enough. "Anyway, I don't care how you spend your fortune. Go away and you will get your share soon." He turned to Adam, "And you get lost too, you old dog."

"I will end the game here. I will not give you your inheritance, nor leave you alive. I have an amazing plan for my dearest brother!"

Adam walked away muttering, "Is this what I get for serving this family for so long? It's true, I am toothless like an old dog. But my former master would never have disrespected me like this. God bless his soul!"

Oliver was alone when Dennis, his servant, came to meet him. "Did you call me, my worship?" he asked.

Oliver asked Dennis whether Charles, the Duke's wrestler, had arrived. Dennis nodded and left to fetch him.

Oliver got lost in thought, "You want to be rid of me, Orlando? This is what you want little brother, then so be it. I will end the game here. I will not give you your inheritance, nor leave you alive. I have an amazing plan for my dearest brother!"

Charles broke his reverie, "Good morning, sir." Oliver greeted him warmly and asked for the latest news from the court. Charles replied, "There is no new news sir, but the same old one. Duke Senior was banished from court by his younger brother, Duke Frederick. So Duke Senior left the court with a few of his loyal lords. Duke Frederick is quite happy with this development. But Duke Senior's daughter, Rosalind, stayed back in the court because of Celia, Duke Frederick's daughter. Celia and Rosalind grew up together and Frederick loves Rosalind like his own daughter."

"So where is Duke Senior now?"

"It seems he's taken up residence in the forest of Arden. Apparently he's living a life of contentment and pleasure, like the people from the Golden Age."

"Hmm," Oliver mulled over this. "Are you still going to fight tomorrow in the court of Duke Frederick?"

"Indeed, sir. In fact, I came here to talk to you about that. I've heard that your younger brother, Orlando, plans to wrestle with me in disguise. You see, sir, tomorrow I am going to wrestle for my pride and reputation in front of the new duke. Therefore, no man shall leave unharmed, I'll make sure of it; it's about my pride.

I am here to warn you, out of affection. You can either stop your brother or be ready to face the disgrace, which shall not be my fault."

Oliver raised an eyebrow and said, "Charles, the truth is, I am aware of my brother's plan and I have tried to reason with him, but in vain. He is a traitor, jealous of other people's wealth, and an overly ambitious man. So, I won't mind even if you break his neck in the fight tomorrow. He deserves it."

Charles bid farewell to Oliver with a resolution to destroy Orlando.

"I hope I'll see the end of my brother soon," thought Oliver, satisfied. "I don't know why but I loathe him. He has never attended school, yet he is intelligent; everyone's favourite and blessed with such gentle manners. Once he is dead, I'll be everyone's favourite."

In the palace, Celia and Rosalind were sitting together in a room, silent and sullen. Finally, Celia spoke, "Rosalind, I have a feeling that you are not happy!"

"Celia, my father has been banished from the kingdom and he is living somewhere in the forest all by himself. How can I be happy?" replied Rosalind.

"If I were you, I would have learned to love your father as mine. Only if you had the same true love for me as I have for you. But, I guess I am not enough for you," Celia frowned.

Rosalind didn't reply. Celia continued, "You know Rosalind, I am the only child of my father. So when he dies, you will automatically receive all his fortune, for everything he has now is your father's. So please, my dear Rosalind, be happy and enjoy these moments with me."

Rosalind smiled and soon they were talking and playing with each other again when the court jester, Touchstone, arrived.

Celia mocked, "Oh, look who's here!"

Rosalind piled on, "I don't think nature wants us to enjoy, or maybe nature thinks that we are not smart enough to have discussions. So she sent this fool to stop us!"

Celia retorted, "Luckily, smart people's wit is enhanced by the presence of such fools." The sisters burst out laughing.

Touchstone humbly said, "Miss Celia, your father wants to see you."

Right then, Monsieur Le Beau walked in. Celia greeted him, "Hello, Monsieur Le Beau, what's the news today?"

Le Beau replied, "Fair Princess, you have missed some good sport!"

"Sport? Of which colour?"

Le Beau was confused. "Which colour? How shall I answer you, Madam?"

"As your destiny dictates."

"Madam, you amaze me. I am simply came here to tell you that you are missing the match going on downstairs."

"How about you tell us the first half, and then we'll decide if we want to watch the next half."

"It's a wrestling match. Charles, the Duke's wrestler, is known for his incomparable strength. No one has ever won against him. Today three brothers came to fight him. Charles overthrew all three brothers and broke their bones! And their poor father was so grief-stricken that the entire audience started grieving for him."

Rosalind gasped, "Oh dear!"

Touchstone said, "But Monsieur Le Beau, first tell us, what are the ladies missing out on?"

Confused, Le Beau replied, "Why, I just told you!"

Touchstone said sardonically, "Men are getting wiser! This is the first time I have heard that rib-breaking was

an appropriate entertainment for ladies." Celia agreed with him laughingly.

"So, shall we see this wrestling?" asked Rosalind.

Le Beau said, "If you choose to stay here, you will have to watch it, for the match is being held here." They all settled in their seats in anticipation.

Rosalind saw Orlando entering the venue. "Has he challenged Charles?" she asked. Le Beau nodded.

Celia observed, "Alas! He is too young for this fight. Yet, he seems capable of it!"

Soon, Duke Frederick approached Celia and Rosalind, "Hello, daughters. Are you here to watch the match?"

Rosalind replied, "Yes, my lord, if you don't mind."

"You are not going to enjoy this match, for the odds are against this young man. I have tried to discourage him, but he isn't ready to listen. Talk to him ladies, he might listen to you."

Celia asked Le Beau to call the young man. Rosalind asked Orlando, "Young man, have you challenged this wrestler for a match?"

Orlando replied, "No, Princess. I am simply here to fight. He is the general challenger. I am here for the same reason other people are—to judge the strength of my youth."

Celia said, "Young man, you are too bold for your age!

You already have proof of this man's cruelty. We beg you to think about your safety and give up."

Rosalind added, "Please, young man, let it go. Don't worry about your reputation, we will personally ask the duke to call off today's match."

Orlando entreated, "Please ladies, don't think poorly of me. I know you're worried about me, but give me your best wishes instead. If I lose, then I'll do so graciously, and if I die then it will be the death of a person who wishes to die. I have no friends to mourn my death. The world won't miss me, for I don't have anything in this world that I can call mine. My absence may be better filled by someone else."

Celia and Rosalind sighed and wished him good luck. Charles called on Orlando for the fight. Duke Frederick said, "You will get only one round to overthrow the other."

Charles taunted Orlando, "A second round won't be needed."

Orlando replied earnestly, “You should wait to mock me until after you have beaten me.”

The fight started; Charles tried to punch Orlando but he was too lithe and quick for him. Suddenly, Orlando tripped Charles, pulled his arm and threw him down.

Duke Frederick got up from his chair and cried, “No more, no more!”

Orlando replied, "Come on, Your Grace, I am barely out of breath."

Duke Frederick turned to Charles. "How are you doing?"

Monsieur Le Beau replied, "He can't speak."

Duke Frederick asked the servants to take Charles away. He then looked at Orlando and asked, "What is your name, young man?"

"My lord, I'm Orlando, the youngest son of Sir Rowland de Bois."

Duke Frederick frowned. "I would have appreciated you if you had a different father. Your father was an honourable man, but he was my enemy. You are a brave man, but I do not wish to see you." The duke and his posse left in a huff.

> "I am proud to be Sir Rowland de Bois' son and I would never change that!"

Orlando called out after him, "I am proud to be Sir Rowland de Bois' son and I would never change that!"

"If I were the duke, I wouldn't have done that!" said Celia, enraged.

Rosalind confessed to Celia, "My father loved Sir Rowland dearly. Had I known that this man is his son, I would have tried harder to stop him."

Celia whispered to Rosalind, "My father's behaviour and rude words are like a sharp knife to my heart. Rosalind, let's talk to the poor soul and encourage him."

They walked up to Orlando. Celia said, "I am very sorry young man, for the duke's behaviour. If you live up to your potential the same way even in your love life, your wife will be the happiest woman alive."

Rosalind looked at him with sympathy and said softly, "Orlando, please keep this chain for good luck. I hope you get what you deserve." Celia and Rosalind left. But Rosalind kept turning back to look at Orlando until he had disappeared from sight.

Orlando stared at Rosalind with surprise and admiration. "I couldn't even say thank you to her. I think my heart has been overthrown ..."

Rosalind felt the urge to speak to Orlando one last time.

She ran back to him. "Sir, you fought bravely. You've conquered more than just your enemy." She blushed and ran back to Celia.

Orlando was tongue-tied. "What is wrong with me?" he thought, "I've been overthrown by something stronger than Charles!"

Monsieur Le Beau approached Orlando and congratulated him on his victory. He hesitated, then said, "Sir, though you fought like a brave man, I request you to leave. Right now, Duke Frederick misconstrues everything you have done. He will not appreciate your presence here anymore."

Orlando replied, "I appreciate your concern, but before leaving I wish to ask: which of the two ladies was Duke Frederick's daughter?"

Le Beau chuckled, "Judging by their manners, neither of them is his daughter; but it is the younger one. The other one is his niece and the daughter of the banished duke. But lately Duke Frederick is not very happy with the attention and pity his niece receives from the people. Soon, his malice towards Rosalind will erupt and she will be thrown out of this palace too. Farewell, sir. I hope we meet in better circumstances."

Orlando gave a curt nod, "I am indebted to you. Goodbye, sir."

Orlando started walking towards the gates of the palace. He sighed heavily, "Out of the frying pan and into the fire—from an autocrat duke to a ruthless brother." He sighed again, "But, oh, heavenly Rosalind!"

Celia and Rosalind were sitting in their room, in deafening silence once again.

Celia broke the spell, "Really? You don't have anything to say to me?" There was a pause.

"I think I have fallen in love with Orlando ..." Rosalind confessed.

Celia raised an eyebrow, "Do you really think it is possible to fall in love so quickly?"

"Well, my father loved his father."

"By that logic, I should hate Orlando, because my father hated his father. But I don't."

"For my sake, don't ever hate him!"

"Why? Does he not deserve it?

Rosalind blushed scarlet, "I love him because he deserves it. You should love him because I do."

Suddenly, Duke Frederick stormed into the room. He thundered, "Rosalind, leave the palace immediately! If I find you within twenty miles of this place, I will have you killed."

Rosalind was appalled. “My lord, please tell me what is my fault? In my knowledge, I haven’t done anything to offend you or your pride.”

Duke Frederick replied, “All traitors say this.”

“But my lord, you cannot call me a traitor based only on your mistrust. This is not just! Please tell me my mistake.”

“You are your father’s daughter. That is crime enough to be punished,” he said.
Celia grabbed her father’s hand and pleaded, “Father, please listen to me ...”

The duke hesitated, but said, "Celia, we kept her here because of you. Otherwise she would have been banished from the palace with her father."

Celia retaliated, "Father, I was very young when you banished him. I didn't beg you to keep her in the palace—it was your decision. Ever since we had been young, we have spent every moment together. I didn't know her value then but I do now. If she is a traitor, then so am I!"

Duke Frederick flared up, "Celia, she is devious! She is grabbing all the attention because of her father and her so-called unfortunate circumstances. I am doing what's best for you. You cannot change my mind; she will be banished." He stormed away.

The cousins wept for a few moments, until Celia declared, "I'll go with you! He has banished me too!"

"No, he hasn't," replied Rosalind.

"Should we part ways then?" Celia whispered.

Rosalind sighed. "But ... where will we go?"

"To the forest of Arden."

"It's far too dangerous for us to travel alone through

the forest."

The women mulled it over and finally Celia proposed that they should wear rugged clothes and put mud on their faces to mask their beauty.

Rosalind had a better idea. "Why don't I dress like a man, since I am quite tall. I can carry a sword and a hunting spear!"

"So what should I call you when you are disguised as a man?" asked Celia.

"Ganymede," Rosalind replied. "What will your name be?"

"You can call me Aliena."

Rosalind suggested that they take Touchstone with them.

Deep within the forest of Arden, Duke Senior and his loyal lords were celebrating their blissful lives as foresters. Duke Senior said, "Friends, I had never thought that I'd be able to experience the true beauty of nature as a result of a most unfortunate incident. Our palace gave us a false sense of comfort, but adversity has given us true knowledge. Away from civilization, I am able to hear the murmur of the babbling brooks, decipher the language of the trees, and discover goodness in everything I see."

One of the lords responded, "My lord, it's astounding to see how wonderfully you have adapted yourself to this environment."

With a smile, Duke Senior asked everyone to come along for hunting.

Back in the palace, Duke Fredrick had called on every servant present.

"How is it possible that no one saw Rosalind and Celia elope?!" he demanded.

A lord replied, "My lord, their attendants saw them going to bed, however, in the morning they'd disappeared!"

Soon, a second lord came in and said, "My lord, your court's clown is also missing."

He added cautiously, "The handmaiden of the princess, Hisperia, revealed that she had heard the girls praising the man who beat your wrestler Charles the other day. It is most probable that the girls are with the same man."

Duke Frederick sent out a town-wide order to search for Orlando. "If you can't find Orlando, then bring his brother, Oliver. I'll make him find his brother."

On the other side of town, Orlando stepped inside his house and was immediately accosted by Adam. "Oh master! Oh my brave master!" Orlando was alarmed at his frazzled state.

Adam cried, "Oh, my boy! Why did you fight that wrestler and showcase your courage? Why are you so virtuous? Why do people love you? Today, your virtue has put you in trouble."

"Adam, what is going on? Why do you look so scared?" asked Orlando.

"Master, Oliver has given orders to burn this house down—with you in it! I eavesdropped on his conversation. He said that if you escape the fire, he'll find another way to kill you, no matter what. I request you, please leave and never come back. This house has nothing to offer you. Your own blood is against you."

Orlando was left speechless. Finally, he said, "But Adam, where will I go and how? I don't have any money! Should I beg?"

Adam said kindly, "Don't you worry, sir. You can use my savings. I had saved the money for my retirement. But now I think you need it more than I do."

Orlando was overwhelmed by the gesture. "Adam, you are truly an amazing person. You're the epitome of old work ethic, when people worked because it was their duty, and not just for money. Please come with me. We'll go together, and instead of spending all your money, we will find another way of living."

Meanwhile, Celia and Rosalind reached the forest of Arden, disguised as Aliena and Ganymede, with Touchstone in tow. They were resting near a waterfall when they saw two shepherds walking towards them.

Rosalind pointed towards them, "Look, the two men seem to be having a serious conversation."

The older man asked with concern, "Silvius, why are you so sad?"

Silvius replied, "Corin, I am in love with Phoebe, but she refuses to accept my love. But you won't understand, since you have never been in love! You've never done ridiculous things for love."

Corin revolted, "I have a thousand times! I just don't remember them."

"Then that is not love!" Silvius replied and stormed off.

Hiding behind the tree, Rosalind sighed, "Oh young man, listening to you, I am reminded of my own pain."

Celia whispered, "Please, can someone go and ask that man if he has some food?"

Touchstone emerged from behind the tree and said, "Hey, you clown!"

"Touchstone, be quiet. He is not your relative!" Rosalind rebuked him.

Corin replied, "Who's calling?"

"Your superiors," replied Touchstone. Rosalind instantly shut him up again and greeted Corin.

"Sir, can you please help us find a place to rest and feed ourselves? We will pay you for the information. We're desperate. My sister here is going to faint; she is starving and tired from travelling."

"Sir, it is a pity," said Corin, "I wish I could help you. If you like you can stay in my master's cottage for the time being. It is empty and on sale."

Rosalind quickly said, "Well, what if we buy the cottage? You can work for us; we'll give you wages." They struck an agreement and started walking towards the cottage.

At the same time, somewhere deep in the forest, Amiens, one of Duke Senior's lords, was singing wildly.

"Under the greenwood tree
Who loves to lie with me?
And turn his merry note
Unto the sweet bird's
throat,
Come hither, come hither,
come hither.
Here shall he see
No enemy
But winter and rough
weather."

Jaques, another lord of the Duke, requested Amiens to continue singing.

Amiens said, "It is only going to make you more melancholy. And my voice is ragged, it will be most unpleasant to hear."

Jaques still pressed him to sing another stanza. Amiens relented, "Fine sir, I'll sing for you. Meanwhile, can you please arrange for a place under the tree for the duke's supper? He has been looking for you since the morning."

"And I have been avoiding him all day," said Jaques. "He keeps trying to argue with me for his own merriment. Anyway, go on, sing."

Close by, Adam and Orlando were treading along the forest floor when Adam stopped abruptly.

"Master, it is impossible for me to walk anymore. I am starving."

Orlando consoled him to stay awake and promised to find some food in the forest.

By now, Duke Senior had met Amiens but was still searching for Jaques. "I am sure Jaques has turned into an animal. Otherwise, I would have seen him wandering about the forest." Amiens said, "Sir, he was here a while ago, listening to songs."

The duke ordered him to find Jaques and bring the man to him. However, Jaques arrived there himself.

The duke asked, "Sir, where have you been all day? Must we beg to spend time with you now?"

Jaques replied cheerfully, "No, my lord! I met a wise fool in the forest! I greeted him, 'Good morning, fool.' He replied, 'No, sir! I am no fool.' He then took out a watch from his pocket and said wisely, 'Right now, it is ten o'clock. Only an hour ago, it was nine o'clock, and within one hour it will be eleven o' clock. This is how we ripen and rot every hour.' Listening to him, I laughed for an hour!"

"Who was this fool?" asked Duke Senior.

"Well sir, he said he was a courtier, but I didn't believe him," replied Jaques.

While Duke Senior and Jaques were talking, Orlando crashed into the clearing with his sword. He pointed the sword at them and said, "Stop! You cannot eat anymore!"

"But we haven't eaten anything yet," Jaques replied.

"And you will not eat till my need has been served."

Duke Senior calmly said, "Well mister, either you're acting brashly driven by tough circumstances or you simply aren't well-mannered."

"Sir, my good manners have been rid of my character by my harsh reality," said Orlando.

"I have been reared well; I don't belong to this forest. But I am forced to squander here," he added.

The Duke shrugged. "So, what do you prefer? You being polite will move us more than you using force."

Orlando sighed, "I am desperate for food. Please let me have some."

"You're welcome to our table," said the duke.

"Such gentle treatment! I apologise for my brash behaviour." Orlando felt embarrassed. "I thought everything here must be wild and severe, and all men animals." Orlando put his sword back into its sheath.

Duke Senior smiled and urged him to eat, but Orlando

said, "Forgive me, but I travel with an old servant of mine who decided to accompany me on this unfortunate journey as a true friend. He is stricken by both old age and hunger. I cannot eat until he has eaten first."

"We will not touch the food until you return with him then," said Duke Senior, and Orlando left.

"Look Jaques," he said, "this proves that we are not alone in our perils. There are other people who are miserable, who we do not cross paths with in our lives."

Jaques leaned against a tree, deep in thought, and said, "All the world's a stage. All men and women are merely actors. A man plays numerous parts in his life. He lives his life in seven acts. In the first act, he is an infant who innocently goes about puking and whimpering in the nurse's arms. Soon, he climbs the ladder of life to become a school boy, with a youthful face, crawling along like a small snail unwilling to go to school. Then, he becomes a lover, sighing over his mistress' mere eyebrow. The fourth act is where he becomes a soldier, with a heavy beard and broad shoulders; ready to save the pride of the country and defend his honour at any cost. In the fifth act, he acts as a judge with all the knowledge gathered from the experiences in his life. With a stern look and a formal beard, he is full of wise opinions. However, in the sixth act, the curtain rises and we see a skinny old man, walking slowly with the help of a stick, and a purse safely at his side full of money earned during his youth. The stocking that used to be tight on his legs now fits loosely on his thin, shrivelled legs. As the play comes close to an end, the hero enters his second childhood—the seventh act. Our hero is forgetful. He has blurred vision, rickety teeth, and only memories to relish. He is a mere puppet whose life ends in nothingness."

Orlando and Adam walked in and broke the sombre spell. Orlando thanked Duke Senior for his generosity, and they sat down for a meal.

Duke Senior said, "If you are actually Sir Rowland's youngest son, as you said, then you're most welcome here. Your father and I were great friends. So I welcome you to my cave along with your old friend."

At the palace, Duke Frederick's soldiers had brought in Oliver. Duke Frederick addressed Oliver harshly, "We have looked everywhere for Orlando. Since we can't find him, we will punish you instead." He ordered his soldiers, "Capture him and seize all his land and assets! Oliver, you have a year to find your brother. If you can't, you will be banished."

In the forest of Arden, Orlando wandered about dazed, muttering to himself, "Rosalind, these trees will be my books which will hold the proof of my love for you. I'll write poems of love and pain on the barks of these trees. That way, whoever passes by these trees will know of the virtuous Rosalind. They will know of my love for you. I will carve praises of your beauty, virtue and unattainability."

In another part of the forest, Corin and Touchstone were discussing life in the forest, when Rosalind, disguised as Ganymede, walked in reading a piece of paper. Touchstone interrupted her and asked, "Sir, if you don't mind me asking, what are you reading?"

Rosalind replied, "I found this poem stuck on the trunk of a tree. It says,

No jewel is like Rosalind.
Her worth being mounted on the wind,
Through all the world bears Rosalind.
All the pictures fairest lined
Are but black to Rosalind.
Let no fair be kept in mind
But the fair of Rosalind."

Before Rosalind could say another word, Touchstone said, "Oh, I could easily rhyme like this for eight years together." Rosalind waved him away. Celia, disguised as Aliena, arrived reading a poem too. It read,

Upon the fairest boughs,
Or at every sentence end,
Will I "Rosalinda" write,
Teaching all that read to know
The quintessence of every sprite
Heaven would in little show.

Therefore, heaven nature charged
That one body should be filled
With all graces wide-enlarged.
Nature presently distilled
Helen's cheek, but not her heart,
Cleopatra's majesty,
Atalanta's better part,
Sad Lucretia's modesty.
Thus Rosalind of many parts
By heavenly synod was devised,
Of many faces, eyes, and hearts
To have the touches dearest prized.
Heaven would that she these gifts should have
And I to live and die her slave.

Celia asked, "Who do you think wrote this?"

Rosalind replied, "I don't know. I think whoever it is, knows me very well."

"And has a chain that once belonged to you."

Celia saw Rosalind's cheeks turn pink. "Are you blushing?" she asked.

"Oh please, Celia! What do you think, who is it?"

Celia sighed and rolled her eyes, "Orlando, of course!"

Rosalind gasped, "Does he know I am here? Did he ask for me? How does he look? What if he doesn't recognise me?"

"It is easier to count atoms than to answer a lover's questions," said Celia, laughingly.

Suddenly, they saw Orlando and Jaques approaching, and hid behind some thick trees.

"Thank you for your company, but I would have enjoyed my own company more," said Jaques.

"I know, but I did it for the sake of good manners," replied Orlando.

"Goodbye then, and let us meet as little as possible."

"Agreed. We are better off as strangers."

Jaques said earnestly, "I hope you won't destroy more trees by carving poems on them?"

Orlando retorted, "Please don't destroy my poems by reading them poorly." There was a pause.

"I don't want to be mean but I don't like the name 'Rosalind'," said Jaques.

"Well, it wasn't meant to please you," said Orlando.

"And how tall is she?"

"As ... tall as my heart," replied the petite Orlando. "I am tired of you and your questions, so I bid you goodbye."

Rosalind, disguised as Ganymede, decided to approach Orlando. Celia tried to stop her, but Rosalind paid no attention to her.

Orlando called out to her, "Who are you, young man?"

Rosalind replied, "I'm Ganymede. I live on the outskirts of the forest with my sister Aliena." Celia walked out from behind the tree too.

"Were you both born here?" asked Orlando.

"Yes, we are very much from here."

"Your language is more refined than I would expect from someone from a remote place like this."

"Many people have told me that. My uncle from the city taught me how to speak. He also taught me about courtship in the city. He strictly preached against it! I'm just glad I'm not a woman ..." said Rosalind.

"Why?"

"Well, it's not just a single reason. According to my uncle, women are, generally, very temperamental. They constantly have new faults to compete with the old ones. He claimed that women keep behaving unexpectedly in situations, which makes them more annoying and incomprehensible."

Orlando was fascinated by Ganymede's words. He said, "Mister, please tell me more."

Rosalind replied, "I am sorry, gentleman. I can't share more just like that. I need to save it for someone who is love-stricken, and for that matter, I have someone in mind."

"Who?"

"Well, there is this man who is carving the trees with the name of his lover—Rosalind. He is destroying the plants by hanging love poems on the branches. He is the one who needs my help."

Orlando confessed, "It's me! I am that unfortunate lover. I want to be cured or I'll drown in my own pain. I cannot explain to you how much I love her."
"Fine, I believe you! I can give you the cure," said Rosalind,

her heart pounding.

Curious, Orlando asked, "Well, how are you going to do that? Have you ever cured anyone?"

Rosalind replied, "I have! Here's how: I disguised as the person's lover and behaved just like her; notorious, filled with too many emotions, longing to be with him. But when I did meet him, I rebuked him; one minute I'd be full of love and the next I'd push him away. His love finally turned into anger, and my work was done. I'll do the same turned into anger, and my work was done. I'll do the same thing with you!" Orlando hesitated, unsure if he wanted to be cured anymore.

Rosalind said gently, "Trust me. I can be your Rosalind. You just have to promise to come and woo me at my cottage every day." Orlando relented and left with a promise to see her soon.

In another part of the forest, Touchstone was walking with Audrey, a local goatherd. Jaques was following them unseen, eavesdropping on the conversation.

Touchstone batted his eyelashes, "Audrey, am I the man of your dreams? Would you like to marry this charming man?"

Audrey replied, "Well yes, I like you for your poetry and your kindness. But I don't believe you are charming. At least not in your features."

Touchstone was taken aback. "What?"

Audrey replied, "Don't mind me! I am not attractive either. So we can definitely get married!"

But Touchstone had different worries. "My love, there is no church here, no priest to get us married. How do we take our vows? Who will declare us as man and wife?"

Jaques revealed himself and said, "Why do you want to marry in a place where there is no church? Hold your horses and wait for the perfect time." Though startled by Jaques' sudden appearance, Touchstone agreed and left with Audrey. Jaques muttered to himself, "God, what were you thinking inflicting such fools on the world! They don't behave like humans. How in the world are they going to live together?"

That afternoon, Celia was resting in their new cottage, while Rosalind was pacing around, waiting for Orlando to arrive.

"My dear sister, stop fretting. He is simply a man you met a few hours ago and whom you know nothing about. He could be chaste, he could be deceitful, he may not be in love at all ..." mumbled Celia.

Rosalind sniffled, "But why wouldn't he come after promising to meet me here?"

Rosalind waited for Orlando desperately. Instead Corin came to the cottage to invite the ladies to see the shepherd they'd enquired after earlier. Rosalind and Celia spotted Silvius and Phoebe in a passionate argument.
Silvius said, "Oh Phoebe, if you want, you can deny my

love for you, but please be kind. You are already breaking my heart by saying no. I request you to reject me kindly. Even an executioner who has seen many deaths, whose heart is now hardened, asks for forgiveness before he executes someone. Will you be crueller than that?"

Phoebe turned away from him, her nose high in the air. "Silvius, I am ignoring you because I don't want to hurt you. You told me that my eyes are murderers. The softest, most vulnerable body parts! They shut at the speck of a dust. What a pretty sentiment! Now, if my eyes are murderers, then you must collapse! Even getting scratched with a tiny pin leaves a mark! When you even lean on something gently, there remains an impression on your palm. But I am looking at you and I can't see a single scratch on your body."

Silvius cried, "Oh Phoebe. Right now you cannot understand my pain. But I am sure, one day when you fall in love with a fair face that holds power over you like you do over me, you will realise my agony."

"Well Silvius, until that day comes, I suggest you stay away from me. You can mock me when it happens. But please don't pity me because until that day comes I won't pity you!" Rosalind couldn't hold her outrage anymore and charged at Phoebe.

Disguised as Ganymede, she demanded, "Well miss, I believe you have a few wrong notions about yourself, so let me clear them one by one. First of all, who do you think you are to be insulting this man as such? What is the reason for your cruel pride? Secondly, you shepherd, why do you run after her? She's nothing extraordinary! It's you who flatters her, not her mirror. And then you two fools will get together and make dull babies. Lastly, your inky eyes and black hair impress no one. I suggest you accept this man's love before you lose out on your slim chance at love."

Rosalind noticed Phoebe staring at her, practically swooning. "Oh lady, please don't look at me like that. Don't fall in love with me. I am falser than a promise made by a drunk man. Do not fall for my anger the way he's fallen for your mocking!" Celia and Rosalind left while the other two stood dumbstruck.

Phoebe turned to Silvius and said softly, "Dear shepherd, now I understand what you meant when you said one can't understand real love until they fall in love at first sight."

"Phoebe, please pity me. I'll do whatever you want."

"Do you know the shepherd who just spoke to us?"

"Not very well. But I have met him several times. He bought the cottage and the land that used to belong to the old peasant."

Phoebe took a deep breath. "Don't think I am in love with this man, Silvius. I just like his build, his eyes, his

complexion and the way he speaks. But when I think about the way he spoke to me, I feel offended. I want to send him a biting letter and insult him. Will you deliver the letter to him, sweet Silvius?" Silvius nodded eagerly.

Later that day, Rosalind and Celia bumped into Jaques. Jaques suggested that they get to know each other better.

With a glint of laughter in her eyes, Rosalind said, "I hear you are a melancholy fellow."

"Well, I do like it better than laughing. So I suppose you've heard right," Jaques replied thoughtfully.

"People who are extreme in either case are no better than drunkards. They have no filter," Rosalind replied.

"I don't have the melancholy of a scholar which is emulation, nor a musician's which is fantastical. My melancholy comes from my travels. When I think of things that I have seen, I experience an almost funny sadness."

"A traveller! Well then your melancholy makes sense. I assume you sold your own land to admire someone else's. And now you have rich eyes but poor hands."

"I am rich in experience."

"And that very experience makes you sad. What use is that?"

Before Jaques could reply, Orlando entered the cottage. "Good day, my dear Rosalind!" he said.

Jaques immediately took their leave, confused by his greeting and wary of Orlando.

Rosalind immediately chided Orlando. "Where have you been? You call yourself a lover? You have insulted me and my time today."

Orlando replied, "Dear Rosalind, I am simply an hour late. If my Rosalind were here, she wouldn't have reacted this way."

"I am Rosalind for now! Come, woo me! What would you like to say to me, your very own Rosalind?"

"I would kiss you first and then talk."

"No! First you talk, and when you run out of words, then you kiss her."
"Well then, as my Rosalind, will you have me?"

"As your Rosalind, I would have twenty such Orlandos. You can never have too much of a good thing! Come, let's be married. My sister can be the priest."

Celia rolled her eyes even as she played along. "Do you, Orlando, take Rosalind to be your wife?"

"Aye. For ever and a day," said Orlando earnestly.

"You should drop the ever and just say 'a day'," Rosalind mock-frowned.

"You see, men are like the month of April before marriage, young and passionate about wooing a girl. But soon after marriage their passion turns into the month of December—cold and unkind. Women are like May when they wed but the sky changes after marriage, uncertain and varying."

"But will my Rosalind do the same?"

"Believe me, she will do as I do." Rosalind supressed her giggles.

"Well, I must take your leave for a couple of hours. I apologise but I have to join the duke for a meal. I'll be back by two o'clock," said Orlando.

Rosalind grabbed his arm. "How do I stay away from you for two hours? Ah! Just go! I knew you were simply a sweet-talker, not a man of his words. How foolish of me! Oh death! Take me away and bring me back to earth at two o'clock!"

"I will keep my promise as if you're my very own Rosalind." With that, Orlando took their leave.

"Time will be the test of that," said Rosalind. And so Rosalind and Celia waited. They waited way past two o'clock, but Orlando never showed up. Rosalind ranted and raged; Celia tried to pacify her, but Rosalind was beyond consolation.

A little while later, Silvius entered the cottage and greeted them. "Sir, I have this letter for you from Phoebe. Pardon me, I am but a messenger."

Rosalind opened the letter and began to read, "'Why have you declared a war on my heart, gentle youth? Your scorning eyes, your chiding and cheeky nature have a strange effect on me.' Wait, Silvius did you write this to mock me? It can't be Phoebe's doing. Well, 'Phoebe' writes, 'I wonder how your mocking, bright eyes have forced me to love you. The one who brings this letter to you is unaware of its contents. Send your answer through him. How I die depends on that answer!'"

Silvius was outraged. "You call this scorning?" he cried.

Rosalind glared at him. "Silvius, do you still love this woman? She has turned you into an instrument and plays lousy tunes on you! Why do you put up with this? I know! Love has turned you tame and unreasonable! I have no pity left for you. Tell her, if she truly loves me, then I'm asking her to love you. I will never accept her as my lover unless you beg me to. Now leave and don't speak to me about this ever again."

As Silvius left, a strange man walked in and said, "I have been sent by Orlando. He has sent his regards and this bloody handkerchief for the boy he calls 'his Rosalind'. Is that you?" He turned to Rosalind, who was still disguised as Ganymede.

Perplexed, Rosalind asked, "What do you mean by the

bloody handkerchief?"

The man sighed, "Bear with me, this is a long story. Orlando was walking through the forest when he saw a young man lying asleep under a tree. Orlando also noticed that a snake had wound itself around the man's neck. The snake was moving towards the man's mouth, but seeing Orlando approaching the snake unwound itself and slinked off into the bushes. But then Orlando saw a lioness hiding by the bushes, watching to make sure he was still alive and waiting to kill the man. Orlando walked closer to the man and realised that it was none other than his elder brother, Oliver!"

Celia intervened, "Oh, I have heard him talk about his brother. Apparently he is the most inhuman man to have ever lived!" The man agreed with her.

But Rosalind didn't care about Oliver. Her heart was stuck on the bloody handkerchief. "Back to Orlando! Did he leave his brother there or did he save him?"

The man replied, "Well, Orlando turned away twice, wanting to take revenge (which his brother certainly deserved). But Orlando's goodness overpowered his want for revenge. He fought the lioness and defeated her! I woke up when I heard them struggling ..."

"Are you the brother? The one who kept plotting to kill

him all his life?" asked Celia.

Shamefaced, Oliver answered, "Yes, that was me. But it's not me anymore. I always hated my brother for being so good and kind-hearted. I always hated him for being more loved than me. Even though he was unschooled and isolated, he was somehow wise and had gentle manners. But, I am happy to be converted. I never believed my brother's pure heart and good intentions. But now I want to make up for lost time."

I never believed my brother's pure heart and good intentions. But now I want to make up for lost time.

"But what about the bloody handkerchief. Where is Orlando?" Rosalind asked.

Oliver replied, "Well, Orlando took me to the duke and gave me a fresh pair of clothes and fed me well. But as soon as he took his clothes off, I saw there was a bad wound on his arm. The lioness had torn a chunk of his flesh away! The blood loss was so much that he fainted, but before that he screamed the name 'Rosalind'."

Oliver continued, "I revived him, and he asked me to find you and beg for forgiveness for not being able to fulfil his promise." Rosalind's knees buckled and she fainted.

Oliver and Celia were able to bring Rosalind back to consciousness after much comforting. They took her by the arm and led her to a chair. Oliver said, "What is this young man? You lack a man's heart!"

Rosalind turned scarlet. "As Rosalind, I was only pretending to faint! It was acting!"

"That was not acting! You've turned as pale as a sheet!"

"It was all pretence, I assure you."

"Well then, pretend to be a man!"

Rosalind laughed, "I am."

"What?" Oliver was taken aback.

Celia hastily ushered Rosalind inside the house, saying she looked paler by the minute. Oliver looked at them suspiciously, but excused himself to get back to Orlando.

Back in the Duke's cave, Orlando was surprised by what

Oliver had just told him. "Brother, I am really happy for you. You're in love with Aliena! It is quite fair to like someone like Aliena, but the question is whether one can like someone at first glance? And in that glance, fall in love with them. And then immediately wish to woo them. And then succeed in wooing them!"

Oliver grabbed Orlando by the shoulders and looked him in the eyes. "My dear Orlando, please don't question the suddenness of my love for Aliena, or my wooing her, or her consenting to my love! Simply support me when I say I love Aliena and she loves me. Besides, I will bequeath unto you all our money. I don't need it anymore. I wish to live the simple life of a shepherd with my Aliena."

Orlando smiled and said, "Well then brother, you have my support. I think you should get married tomorrow. I'll arrange for everything and invite the duke and his lords as well. Now, go get your Aliena, for here comes my Rosalind." While Oliver and Aliena were deep in wedding discussions, Orlando and Rosalind observed them in this new light.

Orlando said, "Life is ironic. I came here looking for my love and Oliver was nowhere close to that feeling. And now, he is getting married and I am the one left alone. It makes me feel bitter to look at the happiness that could

have been mine. I'm happy for my brother, but I am sad for myself. Tomorrow will be the depth of my misery."

Rosalind suggested, "Well then, can I not act like Rosalind tomorrow as well?"

Orlando shook his head. "My dear Ganymede, we cannot live this lie forever. I can't pretend anymore. Someday I have to get married, and it will be to the real Rosalind and no one else."

"Orlando, hear me out now. I have a secret—I have magical powers. I have been trained under a magician since I was three years old. If you wish, I can bring Rosalind here for you. I promise you, you will be married to your dearest Rosalind tomorrow. So invite your close ones and prepare for your wedding!" Orlando's eyes were wide with suspicion and wonder, but he nodded hopefully.

"I have a secret—I have magical powers. I have been trained under a magician since I was three years old."

Silvius and Phoebe also arrived there and Rosalind sighed, "Here comes a woman who loves me and a man who loves her. What a day this is!"

Phoebe stormed towards Rosalind. "You cruel man, why on earth would you read my letter out loud in front of everyone?"

Rosalind replied, "Well, I don't care if you find it rude. I'm simply doing what I feel is right. How can you not see the love for you in Silvius' eyes? I fail to understand the level of ignorance and arrogance you have, lady."

Phoebe turned to Silvius and said, "Silvius, please explain to this young man over here the meaning of true love and respect."

Silvius sighed, "It is to be full of tears and sighs, it means to be loyal and selfless to your love—like I am for Phoebe."

Phoebe looked at Rosalind with doe eyes. "Like I am for Ganymede."

Orlando said, "And I am for Rosalind."

Rosalind piped up, "And I am for no woman!"

Phoebe demanded, "If you know all of this is true, why do you doubt my love for you? Why do you blame me for loving you?"

Silvius glared at Phoebe and said, "And why do you blame me for loving you?"

Orlando jumped in, "And why do you blame me for loving you?"

"Who are you talking to?" Rosalind asked, her forehead wrinkled in confusion.

"To the girl who isn't here," replied Orlando.

Exasperated, Rosalind cried, "Fine! I want you all to remain silent, you sound like a pack of howling wolves. Now, Silvius, I'll help you if I can. I promise to give you what you desire tomorrow. Phoebe, if I ever marry a woman, which will never happen, but if I do, then it will definitely be you. And I will be married tomorrow. My dear Orlando, I will satisfy you, and you will also be married tomorrow. If you really love the people you claim to love as much, please come back here tomorrow. Rest assured, all your dreams and desires will be fulfilled tomorrow. I will not let anyone leave here unhappy."

Everyone nodded in agreement. Rosalind and Celia left for their cottage.

The next day, everyone was abuzz. Duke Senior asked Orlando if he trusted Ganymede. Orlando answered, "Well duke, sometimes I believe him and sometimes I don't. But while one is afraid, there is hope for something better, and the same way, with hope comes fear. For me,

it's a leap of faith which I have decided to take for my love and my life—Rosalind."

Soon, "Ganymede" arrived and addressed the gathered crowd of lovers, "Do all of you promise to keep your word no matter what?" Everyone nodded, still unaware of what was coming. Rosalind asked Duke Senior, "Do you promise to give Rosalind's hand to Orlando if she appears here?"

Duke Senior replied, "Yes, even if I have to give away all my kingdoms with her."

She asked Orlando, "Do you promise to marry his daughter if I bring her here?"

Orlando replied, "Yes I will, even if the duke offers me all his kingdoms instead."

"Phoebe, do you promise to marry me, if I am willing? And if you decide not to marry me, will you marry the shepherd boy, Silvius?" asked Rosalind.

"Yes, even if I have to die an hour later!" Phoebe replied.

"Silvius, if Phoebe is willing to marry you, will you have her?" asked Rosalind.

"Even if marrying her meant death for me!" he replied.

Rosalind smiled mischievously. "I have promised to make everything right, and I will. Duke Senior, I want you to stand by your promise and give your daughter's hand to this young gentleman. Orlando, please keep your promise to marry his daughter. Phoebe, I want you to promise that you will marry me, or marry Silvius if you choose to refuse me. And Silvius, you have to marry Phoebe if she refuses to marry me. Now I am leaving to fetch the answers to all your questions. Please prepare to have your lives changed forever—for better or for worse." Rosalind and Celia walked away, leaving everyone tingling with anticipation.

Duke Senior turned to Orlando and said, "I don't know why but this boy's charisma and personality reminds me of my own daughter."

Orlando agreed with him, "Yes, my lord, the first time I saw him I thought he's Rosalind's brother, but he claims to be a forester who was born and brought up in these woods. His uncle, who lived in the city, taught him these gentle mannerisms and excellent language. Apparently he's a great magician, and he passed his skills on to his nephew."
Soon, Touchstone and Audrey also joined the crowd and

greeted everyone. Jaques grabbed Touchstone in wonder and exclaimed, "My lord, please meet this gentleman! This is the man whom I met in the forest several times. He claims he is a courtier."

Touchstone replied, "Greetings Jaques, it's nice to see you again! And I can prove that I am a courtier. I have flattered a lady, walked a mile, been political with a friend, and smooth with an enemy; I have bankrupted three tailors and been in four quarrels out of which one I fought on seven different levels. But I ended the argument by effectively using 'if'. As in, if the man I'm arguing with said this then I, in response, said this. The argument essentially never happened. We made the whole argument this way and then shook hands and parted ways."

Jaques burst out laughing, "My lord, I like this fellow a lot!"

Duke Senior nodded while chuckling, "I like him as well! He seems like a mere foolish clown but he has deadly wit."

In that moment, Hymen, the God of Marriage, glided in dressed in a flowy white gown. He announced,

"Then is there mirth in heaven
When earthly things, made even,
Atone together.
Good duke, receive thy daughter.
Hymen from heaven brought her,
Yes, brought her hither,
That thou mightst join her hand with his
Whose heart within his bosom is."

Rosalind walked in, followed by Celia, both back to their old selves. Duke Senior gasped, "Am I dreaming or are my eyes deceiving me?"

Orlando sighed, "Oh my Rosalind, I've waited for you for so long. I don't have words to express how I am feeling right now."

Rosalind hugged her father. "I give myself to you for you are my father."

She turned to Orlando and blushed deeply. "I give myself to you, for I am yours and I choose you."

"If my eyes can be trusted, then you are my daughter!" Duke Senior exclaimed happily.

"If my eyes can be trusted, then you are my love!" Orlando gently took her hand.

"Well, if my eyes can be trusted, then I say farewell to my love," Phoebe groaned.

Hymen said in a commanding voice, "Peace! I am here to unite eight lovers with the ones they deserve. Rosalind and Orlando, nothing can part you. Oliver and Celia, you two are united by true love. Phoebe, you must take Silvius as your husband, unless you'd rather be married to a woman. Touchstone and Audrey, you go together like winter and bad weather. Now, without further ado, satisfy your curiosity with questioning. Your surprise will fade when you learn how all this happened."

"I will not go back on my word. I accept you as mine, Silvius," Phoebe said earnestly. Silvius was over the moon! Duke Senior greeted Celia warmly.

While everyone was rejoicing their reunion with their loved ones, Jaques de Bois, Oliver and Orlando's brother, came in and announced, "My dear friends, please listen to me. I am Jaques de Bois, the second son of Sir Rowland de Bois. I have great news for everyone. Duke Frederick, the younger brother of Duke Senior, had prepared a large army when he heard that the duke and his lords were residing in this forest; he planned on defeating his elder brother for good. However, he met an old religious man at the edge of the forest. After speaking to him for a while, Duke Frederick decided to not only abandon the pursuit of his brother but also restore everything he took from his elder brother. He is restoring all the men he exiled during his reign as well, and he is retiring from the world."

Duke Senior exclaimed, "Young man, you have brought brilliant news on this blissful day! Now, I request you to please join us in our celebrations. The fortune can wait; I will bestow it upon those who stayed by my side."

Jaques, the duke's lord, interrupted him, "Wait a minute, sir. Are you trying to say that Duke Frederick has abandoned the throne for the life of a monk?"

"Yes, he has," replied Jaques de Bois.

"Then I will go find him! There is much to be learned from these dramatic transformations."

"We will speak of worldly matters later. Let us finish what we started here and celebrate these young lovers!" declared Duke Senior.

Rosalind walked away from the party and Orlando followed her. "Rosalind, what's wrong?" he called out to her.

Rosalind smiled up at him. “Nothing at all. Orlando, look at what a beautiful sight this is. Lovers united, dancing in contentment. I never imagined I’d end up altering our lives this way. I feel significant and loved. You are with me, and they are with the ones they love—what a blissful life to live.”

Rosalind and Orlando looked into each other’s eyes and finally, they kissed for the very first time.

All the world's a stage,
And all the men and women merely players.
They have their exits and their entrances,
And one man in his time plays many parts.

– **Jaques**, Act II, Scene 7

As You Like It

As You Like It by William Shakespeare was written between 1598 and 1600 and first published in 1623 in Shakespeare's First Folio. It was supposedly first performed in 1603. The play has a pastoral setting that amusingly depicts the two main themes: love and disguise.

Love is the central theme of the play that leads to every action in the story. Shakespeare has very cleverly depicted several perceptions and presentations of love in the play. *As You Like It* has more songs and poems than any other play by Shakespeare, a sign of Shakespeare's enjoyment while writing the play.

The central themes of the play are the delights and drama of love, and country life versus city life. The other themes at play are contrasting families, gender, transformation, art and culture, philosophical viewpoints, and foolishness and folly.

Themes

Love

Love is the central theme of the story that influences nearly every action of every character. The central characters tumble headfirst into love, which is articulated through poetry on tree trunks and sighs. Apart from the romantic and courtly love of Rosalind and Orlando, Shakespeare has also portrayed sisterly and brotherly love through the pairs of Celia-Rosalind and Orlando-Oliver. Another type of relationship depicted by the writer is the fatherly love of Duke Frederick towards his daughter Celia and Duke Senior's towards Rosalind. All these pairs juxtapose one another in the kind of love they're portraying. Rosalind and Celia's love is unconditional and irrevocable, while Orlando and Oliver's starts out as pure hatred and develops through the text consequentially.

The play also deals with the theme of unrequited love and its trials through characters like Phoebe and Silvius. While all the other couples were happy to unite with their beloveds, Silvius and Phoebe's love story ends on a somewhat unsatisfying note as Phoebe marries Silvius only because of her unrequited love for and promise to Ganymede.

Disguise, Deception and Gender

The story is entirely run by the act of deception and disguise, which unfolds the story and provides great comic relief. While the disguises of Celia and Rosalind cause quite a stir amongst the rest of the characters, there can be no doubt about the love between them, since it survives all the deception indulged in by the characters. The disguises also help the characters eventually get their deserved partners and endings.

It is possible that Shakespeare was attempting to mock the gender norms established by the society. For example, Rosalind's disguise as Ganymede lets her experience the world of a man, which she survives just fine, showing that the gender "norms" are very much adaptable and malleable. Despite the constant insinuation that women are temperamental and vulnerable, it is the two main women in the play who run the entire plot and justly determine the fate of all the characters.

Answer me

Q1. What genre would you place this story in and why?

Q2. Write a brief character sketch of Rosalind and Celia.

Q3. Describe Duke Senior's life in the Forest of Arden.

Q4. How does Rosalind come to know that Orlando has also taken refuge in the forest?

Q5. According to you, what was the turning point of the story?

Q6. Rosalind is melancholy at the beginning of the story. Why?

Q7. Why did Rosalind and Celia take responsibility to make all the couples in the story happy?

Q8. What was the effect of the wrestling match on Rosalind and Orlando?

Q9. Rewrite the beginning of the story in not more than 300 words.

Q10. While Duke Senior and his lords resided in the Forest of Arden, do you think it caused any disturbance to nature?

Q11. Shakespeare attempts to portray different characters through a single person in *As You Like It*. Explain with examples.

Q12. List some of the features of a Shakespearean comedy. Do you think *As You Like It* is a typical Shakespearean comedy?

Q13. Briefly describe the character of Touchstone.

Q14. Describe the relationship between Rosalind and Celia.

Q15. Describe how Rosalind and Orlando's affection for each other develops through the story.

Q16. Introduce a new character or plot and rewrite any part of the story in not more than 500 words.

Q17. Oliver was attacked by a wild animal and Orlando saved him. How do Rosalind and Celia find out about this incident? Explain in detail.

Q18. Under what circumstances does Rosalind agree to marry Phoebe?

Q19. "All the world's a stage. All men and women are merely actors. A man plays numerous parts in his life. He lives his life in seven acts. In the first act, he is an infant who innocently goes about puking and whimpering in the nurse's arms. Soon, he climbs the ladder of life to become a school boy, with a youthful face, crawling along like a small snail unwilling to go to school. Then, he becomes a lover, sighing over his mistress' mere eyebrow."

Who said this and why? Do you agree with the statement?

Q20. Do you think Adam played an important role in Orlando's life?

Q21. Do you think Oliver deserved a happy ending? Give reasons.

The end.